W9-AXW-355

HAPPY to be GiRLS

Sarah Davies

illustrated by
Jenny Mattheson

G. P. Putnam's Sons

Bright girls,

Fun girls,

soaking up
the sun girls.

Singing.

Swinging.

Barefoot-in-the-springing.

Big girls, Strong girls,

Playing all day long girls.

Riding. Gliding.

Buried-treasure-hiding.

Great girls,

Brave girls,

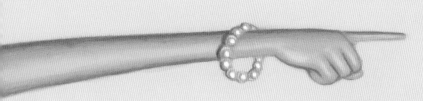

Often misbehave girls.

Fighting. Frighting.

Stay-up-half-the-nighting.

Wild girls,

Free girls,

Happy as can be girls.

Sailing.

Bailing.

sliding down

the railing.

Smart girls,

Icky, sticky

art girls.

Inking.
Plinking.
Sit-around-and-thinking.

Loud girls, Proud girls,

Stand out in a crowd girls.

Being just themselves—

Just

To Su-Ellen,
because every girl needs a very best friend.—S. D.

To my sister Emily.—J. M.

G.P. PUTNAM'S SONS
A division of Penguin Young Readers Group
Published by The Penguin Group
Penguin Group (USA) Inc., 375 Hudson Street, New York, NY 10014, U.S.A.
Penguin Group (Canada), 10 Alcorn Avenue, Toronto, Ontario, Canada M4V 3B2
(a division of Pearson Penguin Canada Inc.)
Penguin Books Ltd, 80 Strand, London WC2R ORL, England.
Penguin Ireland, 25 St. Stephen's Green, Dublin 2, Ireland (a division of Penguin Books Ltd.)
Penguin Books India Pvt Ltd, 11 Community Centre, Panchsheel Park, New Delhi - 110 017, India.
Penguin Group (NZ), Cnr Airborne and Rosedale Roads, Albany, Auckland, New Zealand
(a division of Pearson New Zealand Ltd).
Penguin Books (South Africa) (Pty) Ltd, 24 Sturdee Avenue, Rosebank, Johannesburg 2196, South Africa.
Penguin Books Ltd, Registered Offices: 80 Strand, London WC2R ORL, England.

Manufactured in China by South China Printing Co. Ltd.
Designed by Marikka Tamura. Text set in Klepto.
The art was done in oil paint on primed paper.

Library of Congress Cataloging-in-Publication Data
Davies, Sarah, 1974—
Happy to be girls / Sarah Davies ; illustrated by Jenny Mattheson. p. cm.
Summary: Rhyming text describes different types of girls and the many things they can do.
[1. Girls—Fiction. 2. Self-esteem—Fiction. 3. Self-perception—Fiction. 4. Stories in rhyme.]
I. Mattheson, Jenny, ill. II. Title.   PZ8.3.D2882Hap 2005   [E]—dc22   2004013727   ISBN 0-399-23983-9
10 9 8 7 6 5 4 3 2 1
First Impression